Harriet's Horrible Hair Day

Kids: Please Don't try This at Home

To my mother and father, Evelyn and Neil Stewart, with love,
and for everyone who dreamed my dream and believed.

To the many people who have walked beside me during my lifetime, offering love, friendship, and support—thank you.
My brother Glen, his wife Carol, and my nieces Marina and Cassidy; Aunt Doris, Aunt Sylvia and Uncle Corbie.
Friends: B. G., Barbara, Brita, Donna, Mary, Nora, Rose, and Susan.

—D. L. S.

To Little Sisters everywhere…and to my sister Nancy,
who inspired me and believed in me…other Big Brothers should be so lucky.

Thanks to my wife Traci, whose love and friendship have made me a better person; to Barbara for turning all my
Bad Hair Days into Great Art Days; to Steve for your friendship; to MaryLee for your love and knowledge.

And a special thanks to my family for all of your wonderful ideas: Mae; Don and Judith; Bob and Babs; Courtney (my other little sister)
and David; Tom and Ted; Susie and Corky; Bob and Vera; Pete; and Betsy, Ryan, and Sarah.

—M. P. W.

Published by
PEACHTREE PUBLISHERS, LTD.
494 Armour Circle NE
Atlanta, Georgia 30324

www.peachtree-online.com

Text © 2000 by Dawn Lesley Stewart
Illustrations © 2000 by Michael P. White

Book and cover design by Loraine M. Balcsik

Manufactured in Singapore

10 9 8 7 6 5 4 3 2 1
First Edition

Cataloging-in-Publication Data is available from the United States Library of Congress

Harriet's Horrible Hair Day

Dawn Lesley Stewart
Illustrated by Michael P. White

To Susie and Corky ....

Happy Hair Day!

PEACHTREE
ATLANTA

Love, *Michael P. White 2000*

Sproing!

A curl popped out of Harriet's nice, neat braid. One wriggly, wavy, horrible curl.

"You look weird,"
Harriet's brother said.

"I know something that'll fix that curl,"
Harriet's sister said. "A mud bath."

Harriet's brother took out the hose
and flooded a patch of the garden.

Harriet sank
down
into the mud puddle
until only her nose showed.

They plastered mud
all over Harriet's hair.

"Yuck!"
Harriet said.

Harriet's sister poured a bucket of water
on her head to rinse out the mud.

When Harriet's hair dried,
another curl popped out of
her nice, neat braid.
Now Harriet had *two*
horrible curls.

"That only made it worse,"
Harriet complained.

"Let's find something
to pull those curls straight,"
Harriet's sister suggested.

Harriet's sister and brother tied fishing lines to her curls...
and then they pulled hard.

"*Owww!*" Harriet wailed.

When they untied the lines,
more curls popped out of Harriet's braid.

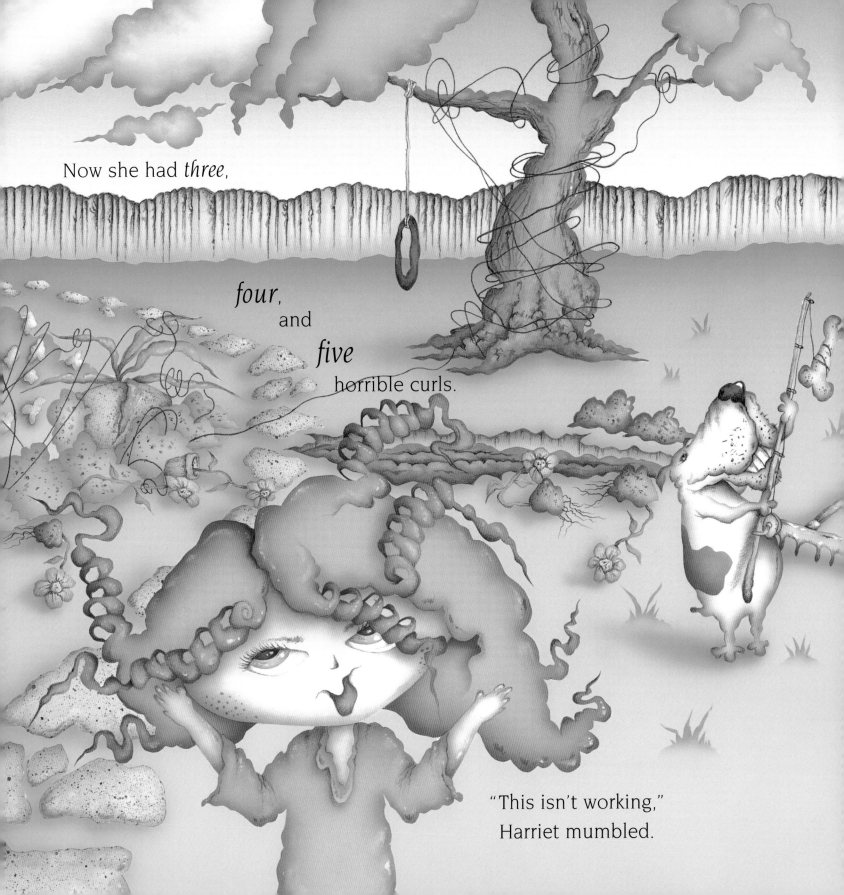

Now she had *three*,

four,
and
five
horrible curls.

"This isn't working,"
Harriet mumbled.

"Hmmm. Let's weigh them down," Harriet's sister said. "Rocks!" she declared.

"And water balloons!" whooped Harriet's brother.

Harriet's head tipped one way
and
then
the other.

"Get these things off!"
Harriet shouted.

When they untied the rocks and burst
the balloons, another curl popped out.
Now Harriet had *six* horrible curls.

"What next?" Harriet muttered.

"C'mon," Harriet's sister said. "Something in the kitchen will work."

Harriet's sister and brother opened the kitchen cabinets and drawers and pulled everything out.

Harriet's sister plopped a colander on Harriet's head, and her brother pulled the curls through the holes.

"Tie the whisk to this curl and
the spatula to that one,"
Harriet's sister directed.

"I can't stand it!"
Harriet grumbled.

When Harriet shoved the colander off her head, three more curls popped out. Now Harriet had *seven*, *eight*, and *nine* horrible curls.

"Aaahhh! Now look what you've done!" Harriet yelled.

"Mom puts stuff in her hair to make it nice," Harriet's brother said.

"We need pickle juice and peanut butter, mustard and molasses," Harriet's sister announced. "And an egg to make it shine."

She squished the goop into Harriet's hair.

"This stinks!" moaned Harriet.

But when
they sprayed the slime
out of
Harriet's
hair…

Now Harriet had *ten*, *eleven*, and *twelve* horrible curls.

"You look weirder than ever," Harriet's brother said.

…even more curls popped out.

Harriet put on her
pajamas, jumped into
bed, and pulled
the pillow
over her head. She tossed
and turned all night.

"Hey, Harriet," her sister called the next morning, "let's pin your curls to the clothesline." Harriet yanked the pillow off her head.

"Go away!" Harriet howled.

"*Wow!*" Harriet's brother said.

"Look at all those nice, neat curls!" Harriet's sister exclaimed.

"You don't look so weird after all," Harriet's brother said.

Harriet smiled.
"I know."